The Bungalo Boys
by John Bianchi
"LAST OF THE TREE RANCHERS!"

It is just after dawn in Beaver Valley, and as the sun climbs into the sky, the Bungalo Boys prepare for another busy day out on the range.

Curly combs his hair.

Johnny-Bob flosses his teeth.

Rufus stacks the breakfast dishes as Little Shorty washes up.
Ma Bungalo keeps a close eye on her boys.

There is no end to the list of the Bungalo Boys' chores.

The stock has to be watered and saddled.

Even Little Shorty lends a hand.

Moving the main herd is no problem. The Bungalo Boys are a seasoned bunch of tree ranchers, the last of a rare breed.

Johnny-Bob, a veteran ranch hand, is quick to rope in a nervous stray.

Little Shorty still has not learned all the ropes.

It's branding time, and the boys find that
putting the famous "double B" on a big one can
be a hot, tough job.

Little Shorty is distracted for just a second and accidentally puts the famous "double B" on the seat of Curly's pants.

Luckily, it's chow time, and the Bungalo Boys turn their attention to a hearty lunch. Ma brings all the fixin's in the chuck wagon, and under her direction, the Boys prepare their own meal. Ma Bungalo has vowed that her boys won't grow up to be helpless men.

Forgetting his manners, Little Shorty eats the last of the pickles — Curly's favourite treat.

"The Triple"

| Tongue-twisting saddle stand | Single-handed limb cling | Backwood head glide |

After lunch, Johnny-Bob shows his brothers some pretty fancy riding. A rodeo champion, Johnny-Bob has mastered the difficult "Triple."

"Careful, Johnny-Bob," shouts Ma. "Don't fall off your tree."

She cautions that only experienced riders should attempt these tricks.

Little Shorty is not allowed.

Later, out on the south forty, the Boys make an unpleasant discovery—rustlers!

"I think I know who's behind this," says Rufus. This time, there is no doubt.

"Yup," says Curly, "looks like the work of the Beaver Gang."

The Beavers have been rustling trees in the valley for a long time, and the Bungalo Boys agree they must find their stock while the trail is fresh.

Eager to help, Little Shorty puts the Bungalos' wonder dog "Projectile" on the scent.

In no time, Projectile has brought the Boys within sight of their quarry.

"There they are, Boys!" shouts Johnny-Bob loudly. He is usually the quiet one.

Little Shorty is quick to give chase.

The Boys spur their mounts into a frenzied gallop and swoop down on the flat-tailed varmints.
   The Beavers panic and make a run for it, but the thundering Bungalo Boys rain on their parade.

Johnny-Bob uses his famous lariat.

Curly chooses a classic tail tackle.

Little Shorty's method is not as smooth.
"Good work," says Rufus. "I'll take it from here."

The Beavers are quickly subdued. But Little
Shorty has skinned his knee quite badly. Rufus
gets the first-aid kit from his saddlebag while
Projectile offers a chocolate-chip dog cookie.

Curly, a budding tree surgeon, does what he can for the recovered stock—most have been badly mistreated. He believes that the Beavers will never change.

"They are nothing but animals," he snorts.

Johnny-Bob — an amateur artist — takes some time to do pencil sketches of the captured criminals. Someday, he hopes to find a publisher for his work.

Night is falling, and the Boys decide to make camp. After supper, Rufus entertains with a tune on his mouth organ. It is hard to resist a Rufus Bungalo harmonica riff, and even the Beavers find themselves singing along.

Little Shorty is chosen to clean up while his brothers relax.

"Ma would be proud of you," says Curly.

When it's time for the Boys to turn in, Little Shorty is chosen to stand guard over the Beaver Gang.

"It will help you learn responsibility," his brothers assure him.

The Bungalo Boys love camping out under the stars and soon fall asleep.

Bored with his task, Little Shorty has slipped away for a quick moonlight ride on Curly's prize thoroughbred, Scotchy. He is sure the Beavers won't even notice he is gone.

Proud of his role in the day's adventure, Little Shorty can't wait until his brothers tell Ma Bungalo how helpful he has been. Gazing up at the moon, he hums a favourite tree-ranching tune:

> "Yippie tie-yie yay,
> get along little sapling.
> The beavers are captured
> And will be chewing no more . . ."